Leader: Martha Singh (supported by Olive Summer)

Age: 13

Status: Billionaire

Company name: HALO

HALO's objective: To carry on the work that Martha's missing mum and dad started – to save wildlife and to save the planet.

Enemy target: TITAN (HALO's enemy). TITAN is a big company that puts wildlife and the environment at risk. It makes money from environmental crime.

Is TITAN behind Martha's missing mum and dad ...?

Next task: Code name: 

Chapter 1

Wiston Hall, England ...

Green Patrol had pizza, but the pizza was getting cold.

"We have a clue about where Martha's parents might be," said Olive.

On a mission to stop a TITAN villain called Lady Varon, Green Patrol had been given a USB stick by a mysterious woman known as Lynx. The USB stick held the entry code to Lady Varon's secret base in the Alps. It also held a top-secret TITAN folder about Martha's parents – Jas and Anna Singh.

On the same mission, Green Patrol had also met Agent Sharp, who was part of a secret group that knew all about TITAN. The secret

HALO

GREEN PATROL

OCEAN

Written by Bali Rai
Illustrated by Margherita Ende

RISING STARS

Hachette UK's policy is to use papers that are natural, renewable and recyclable products and made from wood grown in well-managed forests and other controlled sources. The logging and manufacturing processes are expected to conform to the environmental regulations of the country of origin.

ISBN: 9781398324183

First published in 2021 by Hodder & Stoughton Limited (for its Rising Stars imprint, part of the Hodder Education Group),
An Hachette UK Company
Carmelite House, 50 Victoria Embankment, London EC4Y 0DZ
www.risingstars-uk.com

Impression number 10 9 8 7 6 5 4 3 2 1
Year 2025 2024 2023 2022 2021

Author: Bali Rai
Series Editor: Tony Bradman
Commissioning Editor: Hamish Baxter
Illustrator: Margherita Ende/Astound US
Educational Reviewer: Helen Marron
Design concept: Julie Joubinaux
Page layout: Rocket Design (East Anglia) Ltd
Editor: Amy Tyrer

With thanks to the schools that took part in the development of *Reading Planet* KS2, including: Ancaster CE Primary School, Ancaster; Downsway Primary School, Reading; Ferry Lane Primary School, London; Foxborough Primary School, Slough; Griffin Park Primary School, Blackburn; St Barnabas CE First & Middle School, Pershore; Tranmoor Primary School, Doncaster; and Wilton CE Primary School, Wilton.

A catalogue record for this title is available from the British Library.

Printed in the United Kingdom.

Orders: Please contact Hachette UK Distribution, Hely Hutchinson Centre, Milton Road, Didcot, Oxfordshire, OX11 7HH.

Telephone: (44) 01235 400555. Email: primary@hachette.co.uk.

group had been watching Green Patrol and now they needed Green Patrol's help.

"TITAN have a new plan," Martha told them, "and Agent Sharp thinks it might involve my parents ..."

Olive showed them a map on the giant screen.

"This is the Indian Ocean," she said.

"What's the mission?" asked Silva.

"TITAN are going to sink an oil tanker that's sailing towards Sri Lanka," said Martha. "The oil will endanger the ecosystem for many years."

"But why would they do that?" asked Shan, horrified.

"Money," said Olive. "TITAN will secretly make the mess and then get billions of dollars to clean it up again."

"And then there's my parents," Martha added quietly.

"Are they part of this mission?" asked Silva.

"Maybe," said Martha, shrugging. "HALO got a report that they'd been seen in Sri Lanka. So, now we have a clue to follow."

"It might be our hardest mission yet," said Max.

"It will be," said Martha, frowning. "But it will be our most important one, too ..."

Green Patrol could see that she meant it.

Chapter 2

Sri Lanka, 24 hours later ...

Green Patrol took a HALO plane to Sri Lanka. They landed by the coast, near a city called Colombo. When they got there, they split up into pairs.

Martha and Shan went to meet Agent Sharp, at a skyscraper hotel by the sea.

"How do we stop the tanker?" asked Martha.

"We're working on a plan," Agent Sharp replied.

Agent Sharp opened a folder on her tablet screen. "This is Lord Carter," she said. "He's from London."

Lord Carter was a dangerous TITAN villain. He was one of the company's main owners and the brains behind TITAN's biggest crimes.

"Max and Ayan are tracking him," said Agent Sharp.

"They'd better be careful," said Martha, after reading Lord Carter's folder. "He's been linked to all kinds of awful crimes – smuggling, kidnapping, forest fires ..."

Martha changed folders on the tablet screen. The new one was for her parents. "What about my mum and dad?" she asked Agent Sharp.

"Olive and Silva are on the case," Agent Sharp replied. "The clue from the USB stick links your parents to Colombo – and to this mission."

"Do you really think they're still alive?" asked Martha.

"Sure, kid," said Agent Sharp. "And we're going to find them!"

Chapter 3

A café on a coastal road ...

Max and Ayan were on the coastal road, not far from Martha and Shan. From a café across the street, they watched Lord Carter get out of his sleek, shiny black car. He was short with wide shoulders and a shaved head. He wore a dark grey suit, white shirt, black shoes, and dark sunglasses. He had two bodyguards with him – a man and a woman.

Lord Carter and his bodyguards crossed the road and sat down three tables away from them. Then, he called someone on his phone, which looked like a child's toy in his massive hands.

"Can we listen to his phone call?" asked Max.

Ayan used her HALO phone to pick up Lord Carter's signal. They could hear every word.

"Listen carefully," Lord Carter growled at someone. "I've changed the plan so no one will find out what we're up to. Not until it's too late ..."

"That's what he thinks," murmured Ayan. "We're going to find out!"

Chapter 4

HALO

A golf course by the sea ...

Olive and Silva were two miles away from Max and Ayan, on a golf course by the sea. But they weren't playing golf. Silva was using his HALO phone to zoom in on a small, white boat out at sea.

"What can you see?" asked Olive.

"Not much," Silva replied.

"Is your HALO phone broken?" said Olive.

"No, it's fine," Silva replied. "But there are no people on the boat."

"How can that be possible?" asked Olive. "Let me look."

She used her own HALO phone to check. Silva was correct. The boat was abandoned. Olive started to become suspicious.

"*Olive* ...?" said Silva.

"Yes, dear?"

"The boat," Silva told her. "It's moving."

Olive zoomed in on her own phone. The boat was moving, the steering wheel was turning, but there was not a single person to be seen on board!

Chapter 5

Back at the skyscraper hotel, Agent Sharp, Martha and Shan were waiting for a message.

"My agents have worked out *part* of the plan," Agent Sharp said.

Shan sipped a cola as Agent Sharp's mobile phone buzzed. Agent Sharp seemed a little surprised.

"It's time to move ..." she said, after replying to the message. Then she smiled.

"What are you smiling at?" asked Shan.

"Have you ever jumped from a helicopter on to a moving boat before?" asked Agent Sharp.

Martha looked surprised. “What’s the plan?” she asked.

Agent Sharp gulped down her coffee. “I’ll tell you on the way to the roof!” she said.

Up on the roof of the skyscraper, a helicopter was waiting. Martha and Shan were going to fly to the oil tanker. Then they would use special winged suits to jump on to the tanker.

“They’re just like gliders,” said Agent Sharp, holding one of the black jumpsuits up.

“I know,” said Martha. “We made them!” She pointed to a HALO logo on the jumpsuit.

Shan wanted to know more about the plan. "So, what happens when we land on the oil tanker?" she asked.

"I'll direct you on your phones," Agent Sharp explained. "I'll be in the helicopter, above the tanker."

"And what if we get caught?" said Martha.

"You won't get caught," said Agent Sharp. "The crew will be resting. The tanker will be on autopilot ..."

"What if we can't stop it?" asked Shan.

"You *will* stop it," Agent Sharp told them. "You are Green Patrol. You *never* give up!"

Chapter 6

HALO

The coastal road ...

Out on the coastal road, Ayan and Max followed Lord Carter from the café. He walked back to his car and then stopped. He seemed to be looking for something out at sea.

"Do you think he's just enjoying the view?" asked Max.

"It *is* wonderful," Ayan murmured longingly. "Reminds me of home."

The view was stunning. The beach was white sand and dotted with palm trees. The water was dark blue and very still, and the sun was like a burning orb and getting lower in the sky. It was like a scene from a postcard.

"He's moving again," said Max.

They followed Lord Carter to a nearby hotel. It was right by the sea and had a private beach with its own bar and café.

Max took out his HALO phone and began to tap the screen.

"What are you doing?" asked Ayan.

"Checking the hotel computer to see if Lord Carter is staying here." Max replied.

He tapped a few more times and found what he was looking for. "TITAN have seven rooms on the top floor of the hotel," he said. "Lord Carter is staying in Room 605. The biggest room in the hotel."

Ayan was confused. "So what?" she asked.

"So, let's go and have a look," said Max.

"We can see if Lord Carter has hidden anything useful in his room!"

Max led the way, and at the hotel front desk, he showed his HALO phone. The woman behind the counter checked her computer screen and then smiled. "You are here to meet Lord Carter?" she said. "Of course. Please go ahead."

Max smiled and walked to the lifts.

"What did you show to the woman?" asked Ayan.

"I hacked the hotel computer," said Max. "It says Lord Carter is expecting us."

"That's smart," said Ayan.

"Only if we don't get caught," Max told her. "Come on!"

Chapter 7

At the golf course, Olive frowned. “We have a problem,” she said.

Out at sea, the boat was still moving away.

“I’ve just checked with the local port,” said Olive. “It shouldn’t be there. There must be a reason why.”

“It’s odd how it’s here, so close to the oil tanker,” said Silva.

A woman who worked at the golf course came over to collect their glasses. She smiled at them and pointed at the boat.

“There was a man,” she explained to Olive and Silva. “He was watching the boat, too, and filming it on his phone.”

Silva got a funny feeling in his stomach.

"Where did the man go?" asked Olive.

"Nowhere," said the woman. "He's in the main building, drinking coffee."

"We should check him out," Silva said to Olive.

They thanked the woman and went to find the mystery man.

The golf club coffee bar was large but almost empty, and most of the white plastic tables had been tidied up. The man looked like a local. He sat on his own, with a tablet computer, watching the screen closely.

"What shall we do?" whispered Silva.

Suddenly, the man stood up and left, and Olive and Silva had to quickly follow.

The man left the golf course, but didn't go far, walking along the road, back towards the sea. When he reached the beach, he took out his tablet computer.

"I'll jog by him," said Silva. "He won't suspect me."

"Okay," said Olive, "But be careful."

Silva was gone for a few minutes. When he returned, he was out of breath. "He's controlling the boat from his tablet," he said, panting.

"But why?" said Olive. "What is the boat for?"

Silva shrugged.

"We had better find out then," said Olive.

Chapter 8

Ayan and Max were on the sixth floor of Lord Carter's hotel.

They walked down the corridor until they found Room 605. It had a security-coded lock.

"One moment," said Ayan. She used her HALO phone to hack the hotel computer and unlock the door.

They quickly searched each room, looking for any clues, but they didn't find a thing.

"What now?" asked Ayan.

"We carry on watching Lord Carter," said Max, shrugging.

Max quickly called Martha to check in, but she didn't reply. "That's odd," he muttered.

Suddenly, the hotel room door opened and Lord Carter stomped into the room, his burly bodyguards towering either side of him.

"Quick!" Ayan whispered.

Max followed her and they crept out on to the balcony.

"What now?" Max whispered.

"*Now*, you tell me what you're doing in my room," boomed Lord Carter. He was standing by the balcony doors with a fierce expression on his face.

Max and Ayan were shocked. How did he know who they were?

"I know everything," laughed Lord Carter, as if reading their minds.

He turned to his bodyguards. "Grab them!" he yelled.

Chapter 9

In a helicopter over the sea ...

Martha and Shan waited for the signal. Then they leaped from the helicopter. There was no wind, so the jump was quick and easy. The special jumpsuits let them glide safely down on to the huge oil tanker.

"That was so cool," said Shan, once they had landed.

"Super cool!" said Martha. "I want to keep one!"

“This ship is massive!” said Shan, amazed.

It was dark, and Martha and Shan couldn’t see anyone. From the helicopter above them, Agent Sharp was using infrared cameras to direct them. “Go left and you should reach an air vent,” she said. “There will be a door and some stairs. Go in and down. Wait at the bottom. The lower deck will be lit.”

Martha led the way. The harsh lights in the stairwell made Shan squint.

“What are we looking for?” asked Shan.

“TITAN plan to blow a hole in this tanker,” said Agent Sharp. “We need to find out how, and then stop it.”

Chapter 10

The coastal road ...

Olive and Silva followed the man as he left the beach.

"I can't see the boat now," said Silva. "It's too dark."

Olive sent a message and got a reply almost straight away. "The boat is being tracked," she told Silva. "It won't disappear."

The man hovered at a small supermarket and looked up and down the street. Olive and Silva were too close – they would be seen. Instead of stopping, they walked on.

"What's he up to?" asked Olive.

Silva turned to look. "He's gone down an alley," he replied.

"Let's follow him," said Olive, as they walked back.

The alley was deserted except for a pile of rubbish and a side entrance to a dingy-looking building.

“He must have gone inside,” said Silva.

“We have to go after him,” said Olive.

The building was dark and had an awful chemical smell. A short corridor led to another door. Voices came from behind the second door.

“I can hear him!” whispered Silva.

The man was talking to someone. Olive and Silva couldn’t see him, but they heard every word. What they heard made their blood run cold …

“Oh, no!” groaned Silva.

“We’d better tell the others,” said Olive. “This changes everything!”

Chapter 11

Lord Carter's hotel ...

Max and Ayan sat on a bed locked in Lord Carter's hotel room. The room had a window, which looked out to sea, and one door. Lord Carter's bodyguards were outside the door. There was no escape. They were trapped.

There was knock on the door. Lord Carter entered.

"Green Patrol," Lord Carter gloated. "I finally have you."

"No, you only have two of us," Ayan snapped. "The rest of our team will stop you!"

Lord Carter laughed. "No one can stop me," he said. "Your friends think they know my plan, but I have changed the plan. Now, tell me what you know!"

"No!" Ayan yelled back.

"Very well," muttered Lord Carter. "I'll give you an hour. When I come back, you will tell me everything."

"What happens if we don't?" asked Max.

"Then you will pay a terrible price!" hissed Lord Carter.

When he had gone, Max turned to Ayan. "We have to escape and alert the others that he's changed the plan," Max told her.

"I know," said Ayan. "But he's taken our HALO phones. Even if we get out, we can't contact the others."

"Our phones are in the living area," said Max. "Maybe we can get them back?"

"How?" Ayan asked.

Max pointed to the window. Ayan smiled.

Chapter 12

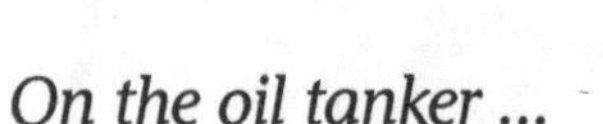

On the oil tanker ...

Out at sea, Martha and Shan had reached the crew's quarters. A narrow kitchen led them into a corridor with cabins on either side. The thick steel cabin doors hung open, and behind each door there were two bunk beds and a bathroom. They were all empty, until the very last one ...

"Oh, no!" Shan cried out.

"What's going on?" Agent Sharp asked over their ear buds.

"The crew," said Martha. "They've been tied up!"

Their mouths had been gagged and they had been bound to their chairs with rope. When they saw Martha and Shan, they tried to speak and move.

"I'll be right back," said Agent Sharp. "Olive is just calling ..."

"Come on," urged Martha. "Let's untie these people!"

Shan moved to the nearest man and attempted to undo the tight knots.

She turned to Martha for help and saw that she was holding her HALO phone, her face had gone pale and her eyes were wide.

"What's the matter?" asked Shan.

"Olive discovered something ..." said Martha. "We have to get off this tanker. All of us. NOW!!"

Chapter 13

The coastal road ...

Olive and Silva ran back into the street. Even though it was late, the street was full of people, cars and taxis.

Despite being shocked by what she'd heard in the building, Olive had already called Agent Sharp. The small boat that she and Silva had been watching was the key to Lord Carter's plan. The boat was loaded with explosives and would reach the oil tanker very soon. When it did, it would blow a hole in the tanker, and millions of gallons of oil would spill into the sea.

But something even worse would happen. Martha, Shan and all the crew on the tanker were in terrible danger – but Martha's parents were tied up on the small boat!

"We've got to stop that boat *NOW!*" yelled Silva, clenching his fists in anger.

"Look – it's the man!" whispered Olive.

The man they had been following came out of the alley. He ignored Olive and Silva and walked away.

"He's got a backpack," said Silva. "His tablet computer will be in it."

"We have to get that tablet!" said Olive.

Silva grinned. "Leave that to me," he said.

Silva jogged towards the man. A group of locals were coming in the opposite direction. Silva sprinted and barged into the man, who fell into the group of locals.

When Silva got back to Olive, he was grinning.

"What did you do?" asked Olive.

"I took his backpack," said Silva, shrugging.

"You *stole* it?" said Olive.

Silva just grinned again. He checked the tablet and shook his head. "No password," he murmured.

He tapped a few commands into the tablet. "This signal is being bounced to a hotel," said Silva. "It's the hotel that Lord Carter is staying at ... Lord Carter is in control of the boat!"

Chapter 14

Lord Carter's hotel ...

Max opened the window of the hotel room and Ayan looked out.

"Er ... it's quite high," she whispered.

"We're six floors up," said Max. "Scared?"

"No way!" Ayan snapped.

Ayan climbed out on to a ledge and then edged towards the balcony. The ledge was narrow, but that did not stop her.

Max followed. "Just don't look down!" he said.

Ayan climbed on to the balcony. Max was right behind her. They crouched and looked into Lord Carter's hotel apartment. It was empty.

Ayan gently slid the balcony doors open. "Wait here," she whispered to Max.

Ayan crawled into the room, grabbed their phones and scuttled back to Max on the balcony. Lord Carter appeared just as she closed the doors, and the two children quietly moved out of his view.

Typing quietly, Max messaged Olive.

"She's on her way here!" he gasped.

"Why?" asked Ayan.

"Lord Carter is controlling a speedboat packed with explosives," said Max, his voice shaking. "And that's not all!"

"What?" asked Ayan.

"Martha's parents are tied up on the speedboat!"

Chapter 15

Outside Lord Carter's hotel ...

Olive called the local police as she and Silva sprinted towards the hotel. At the entrance, Olive checked her HALO phone. "We have less than ten minutes," she told Silva. "Come on!"

As they waited by the lifts, the local police arrived and Olive told Police Chief Jasmine Fox what was going on. Jasmine looked enraged. She ordered her officers to seal off the hotel. No one would be allowed to leave.

"Time for Lord Carter to pay for his crimes!" she announced to Olive and Silva.

Olive's fingers trembled as she called Agent Sharp.

"We don't know how to stop the boat," said Agent Sharp grimly.

"That's no good!" yelled Olive.

On the balcony, Ayan tried to take control of the boat from her HALO phone. If she could do that, she could stop it.

"How long will it take?" said Max.

"It's quite hard," Ayan snapped, tapping away frantically. "Give me a minute ..."

"Hurry up!" said Max.

He checked his own phone and saw that Olive had placed a tracker on the small boat. It was getting closer and closer to the oil tanker ...

"*Nearly* there ..." muttered Ayan. "Just one more ... GOT IT!"

Chapter 16

On the oil tanker, Martha and Shan explained the situation to the dazed crew.

"There's a boat coming this way!" Martha told them. "It will blow a hole in the tanker. We have to leave!"

"You have eight minutes ..." said Agent Sharp in their ear buds. "Get to the deck. I have helicopters coming for you."

"But what about my parents?" Martha asked.

"We're doing everything we can," Agent Sharp replied. "Now, hurry!"

Martha took a deep breath and pulled herself together. She turned to the crew. "MOVE!" she yelled.

Martha and Shan followed the crew up to the deck where two HALO helicopters were already landing.

"GO! GO! GO!" Martha yelled.

The crew jumped aboard the helicopters and the helicopter blades whirred into action. Within a minute, they were clear of the oil tanker.

Agent Sharp's helicopter landed to pick up Martha and Shan, and soon they were clear of danger, too.

"Where's the boat carrying my parents?" yelled Martha.

"Two minutes away," replied Agent Sharp.

"And the rest of Green Patrol?" asked Shan.

"Dealing with Lord Carter," Agent Sharp told them. "I just hope they're not too late ..."

Chapter 17

Back at the hotel, Olive, Silva and the police burst into Lord Carter's room.

"You meddling brats!" bellowed Lord Carter. "You can't stop me!"

Olive shook him by the shoulders, as the police officers handcuffed him. "STOP THE BOAT FROM EXPLODING!" she yelled.

"I can't stop it," he said. "It doesn't matter anyway."

The HALO helicopter carrying Martha, Shan and Agent Sharp sped towards the boat.

Agent Sharp had a heat sensor aimed at the boat, which would show them exactly where Martha's parents were.

"That's very odd ..." said Agent Sharp. The rest of her sentence was lost.

Without warning, the small boat exploded, sending flames, smoke and wreckage high into the air. Martha screamed as the pilot veered away, jolting everyone in their seats.

"MY PARENTS!" Martha sobbed.

"But there weren't any heat signatures on the boat!" said Agent Sharp.

"What?" replied Martha. "But you said my parents were on board ..."

"We must have been wrong," said Agent Sharp. "Your parents can't have been on the boat after all!"

Martha just stared at her, stunned ... "But then, where *are* they?"

Chapter 18

Wiston Hall, England ...

After the mission, Agent Sharp joined Green Patrol in Martha's kitchen. But, no one had much of an appetite for pizza.

"I don't understand," said Martha. "My parents weren't on the boat that exploded. Why did the TITAN report get that wrong?"

"It didn't," said Agent Sharp. "Lord Carter told us after we arrested him that TITAN had sent the fake report to HALO."

"So, my parents were never on the boat?" asked Martha. She looked relieved.

"No," said Agent Sharp. "TITAN were trying to distract you from our mission. But the good news is that your parents are alive. And they were in Sri Lanka – we've checked. We just don't know why, or where they are now."

On the big screen, Agent Sharp showed them photographs of Martha's parents, taken in the days before their mission. They were walking down the coastal road in Colombo.

"That's definitely them," said Martha. "But why haven't they contacted me?"

Agent Sharp shrugged. "We don't know," she said. "But we *will* find them."

"We have to find Martha's parents," said Ayan.

"Yeah," said Max. "We didn't complete the mission this time. We failed ..."

"We didn't fail," Martha told them. "We just didn't find my parents. They went missing long before Green Patrol appeared. You did awesome work!"

Martha sounded strong but the look in her eyes gave her away.

An image flicked on to the screen. They could see a tropical island, surrounded by azure-blue seas. It looked like an image of paradise.

"No ...!" moaned Max, Ayan and Silva together. "Not *another* mission!"

"Oh," said Olive. "You will *love* this one. There's a beach and lots of rare animals and nature ..."

"What plan have TITAN got this time?" asked Shan.

"No plan," said Olive. "This is where you are going on holiday!"

Green Patrol looked at each other in shock.

"You mean we get to rest?" Ayan gasped.

Martha and Olive nodded. "Just for a short time," said Martha.

As she spoke, Martha received a message on her HALO phone from an unknown number. Unsure, she opened the message – and nearly dropped her phone in shock. It was a photo of her parents, waving! It looked like they were somewhere in India. The message read:

YOU HAVE MADE US SO PROUD. NEVER GIVE UP! WE'RE CLOSER THAN YOU THINK. YOUR COUSIN, OLIVE, WILL EXPLAIN EVERYTHING! ALL OUR LOVE, MUM & DAD XX

Martha was stunned. *Her parents really were alive ... They knew about her work with Green Patrol ... and she was related to Olive!* It was so much information to take in. Her heart fluttered with a strange mixture of joy and nerves.

She looked up to see Olive checking her own HALO phone. Olive caught her gaze and winked at her, before speaking to the rest of Green Patrol.

“Martha and I have a mission of our own to attend to,” she said.

“What’s the job?” asked Ayan.

“Mission: Reunion,” Olive grinned. “For the rest of you, TITAN is still out there, which means there will be more crimes to stop. Have a rest, enjoy your break and then be ready for my call.”

Ayan yawned. Max grabbed another slice of pizza. Shan smiled.

“No problem,” said Silva. “We are Green Patrol. We never stop. And we *never give up!*”

Chat about the book

1. How did Shan and Martha get on to the oil tanker?
2. Lord Carter's bodyguards are described as 'burly'. What other words could have been used by the author?
3. Go to page 20. Why do you think Silva had a funny feeling in his stomach?
4. Chapter 10 ends with Olive saying "This changes everything". Why is this a good way to finish the chapter?
5. Read Chapter 17. How did Agent Sharp and Martha react when the boat exploded?
6. Do you enjoy stories like '*Green Patrol: Ocean*' that have an environmental theme? Why or why not?